# WILL THE WORD EATER

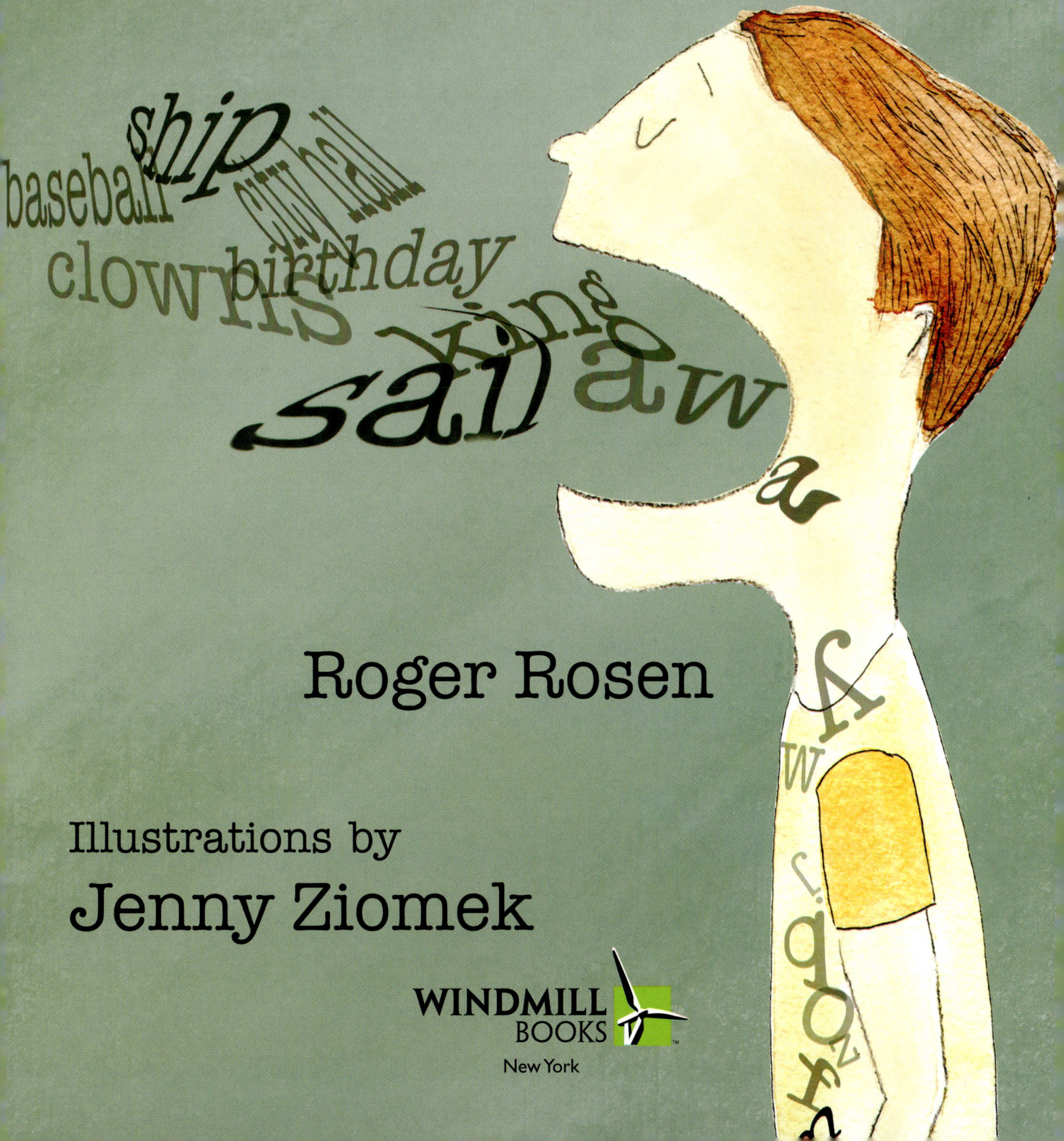

Roger Rosen

Illustrations by
Jenny Ziomek

WINDMILL BOOKS
New York

Published in 2021 by Windmill Books, an Imprint of Rosen Publishing
29 East 21st Street, New York, NY 10010

Copyright © 2021 Text Roger Rosen, Illustrations Jenny Ziomek

All rights reserved. No part of this book may be reproduced in any form without permission in writing from the publisher, except by a reviewer.

Cataloging-in-Publication Data
Names: Rosen, Roger, author. | Ziomek, Jenny, illustrator.
Title: Will the word eater / Roger Rosen, illustrated by Jenny Ziomek.
Description: New York : Windmill, 2021.
Identifiers: ISBN 9781725394292 (pbk.) | ISBN 9781725394315 (library bound) | ISBN 9781725394322 (ebook) | ISBN 9781725394308 (6 pack)
Subjects: LCSH: Vocabulary–Juvenile fiction. | School–Juvenile fiction. | Families–Juvenile fiction.
Classification: LCC PZ7.R674 Wi 2021 | DDC [E]–dc23

Manufactured in the United States of America

CPSIA Compliance Information: Batch #BWWM21 For Further Information contact Rosen Publishing, New York, New York at 1-800-237-9932.

My Dad eats words for breakfast.

I do too.

His words are on his phone.
He washes them down
with black coffee.

I like to make words
on the table.

PONY.
BASEBALL.
My name, WILL.

I put them in my
cereal and watch
them float.

Sometimes I want to share a word with my Dad.

"Hey, Dad, look: BASEBALL."

He never looks.

Dad only wants to share his words with my mom.

"Hey, Steff. Can you believe this clown in City Hall? Can you believe it?"

He talks a lot about clowns.

My Dad eats words because they make him strong.

He also likes to spit them out.

He likes to poke them with his finger.

Or Tweet them.

I put Sam's name in my cereal. Sam is my best friend. But yesterday he told me to *shut up*.

I was telling him a story about my dad.

So I shut up.

I grabbed the words I wanted to say and stuffed them into my shirt.

But the words didn't want to stay inside.

They kept flapping around,
jumping this way and that.

And the tighter I held on, the more they wanted to pop out.

I don't want to go with Sam to school today.
I'm worried about the words that will pop out.

So I say them to my dad instead.

I say, "I hate school."

Right away, I want to take those words back.
I want to eat them myself.
I want to crunch them with my teeth.
I want to make sure they don't escape.


But it's too late.
I can see them going down into his belly.

When my Dad opens his mouth,
I can see my words in there.

"You hate school?"

Dad's words rush out of his mouth.
I can see a lot of others too.
They are waiting in line to come out.

CLOWN

CITY HALL

SAY PLEASE

NOT SO FAST

LITTLE BOYS
DON'T GET TO DECIDE

All those words coming out of his stomach make his eyebrows come together.

Mom says, "But you used to love school!"

Dad says, "You don't know how good you have it."

So I shut up again.

I walk to school with Sam.
I want to ask him if his dad
always talks about clowns.

But I don't open my mouth.
I don't know what would come out.

Sam sits next to me at the special assembly. He asks me, "Who's that with Mr. Evans?"

I say I don't know.

Maddie Winters tells us, "That's Tyler Adams, the famous author. Don't you know anything?"

Mr. Adams begins to read, "And the ship set sail..."

And his words rush toward me on a wave.

I swallow them and then the ship begins to sink.

I don't know if the ship is sinking in Mr. Adams's story. In my story, the one my brain makes as he talks, the ship is sinking.

I'm scared there is going to be a quiz.

I ask Maddie, "Is the ship sinking?"

"Shh," she says.

In class, Mrs. Day asks us
to write a story about a ship.

Maddie Winters asks, "On the sea?"

"If you want," Mrs. Day tells her.

I ask Mrs. Day,
"What color does the ship have to be?"

"Whatever color you want it to be," she says.

Then I ask, "Who is allowed to be on the ship?"

"Whoever you want to be on the ship," she says.

This makes me feel better. It makes me feel free.

I have a story to tell.

We have to choose a writing buddy.

I tell Sam, "The white ship is sinking."
He looks at me funny.

"You want to start the story that way?"

"I don't know," I say. "Why not?"

Sam says, "If the ship sinks on the first page, what are we going to write on the second page?"

I tell him, "Maybe the ship sinks because the captain of the ship is a clown."

"A clown?" Sam asks. "That's a dumb idea."

"No, listen," I say. "Once upon a time there was a king who had a law that children could not have birthdays or birthday cakes. Only the clowns of the kingdom could eat the cake."

Sam says, "I'm not going to write that down."

"But–"

"Shut up."

Then Tyler Adams visits our class.
"What are you writing about?" he asks.

I want to tell him all the words that are rushing to get out. They're pushing against each other to be the first ones to leave my mouth.

Maddie Winters says she's writing about a ship on a stormy sea. "Good idea," Tyler Adams says.

He asks if we have any questions for him.

I raise my hand. I ask Tyler Adams, "Did anyone ever tell you to shut up?"

Tyler Adams smiles. "One day, at the playground, this bully said to me, 'I'm going to make you eat those words.'

And I said, 'I don't think so.' I've been turning my words into stories ever since."

My dad eats words for breakfast.

I write stories.

Sometimes I read them.

Sometimes my dad listens.

"Once upon a time there was a king who had a law that children could not have birthdays or birthday cakes. Only the clowns who ruled the kingdom could eat cake. So on one stormy night, when no one was looking, all the children sailed away..."

My dad says, "That reminds me of all the clowns we have in City Hall. I wish they would sail away.

That's a good story, son!"

I watch my dad's words float in my cereal.

And then I pick up my pencil and set my words free.